The Nicholas Stories

The First Flight of Saint Nicholas

Written by Harry B. Knights

Original Artwork by Calico Studios

Publisher - Lacey D. Faw

Zweig Knights Publishing

A Subsidiary of Studio City Holding Corp.

Limited 1st Edition

Registered Number: 4929

10,000 limited first editions published; November 1, 1998

The Nicholas Stories

To Nicholas...

Remember...

Always Believe!

Danny B Knight

3/2/2002

1

The Nicholas Stories
The First Flight of Saint Nicholas

Written by Harry B. Knights

Original Artwork by Calico Studios

Publisher - Larry D. Faw

Zweig Knights Publishing

A Subsidiary of Studio City Holding Corp.

Dedication
To my mom and dad, Betty and Harry.
I love you both and thank you for teaching me
to love Christmas. You helped make these stories possible.

ISBN: 1-58114-002-9

Cataloging-in-Publication Data

Knights, Harry B.

   The Nicholas Stories: The First Flight Of Saint Nicholas

     P.cm

Summary: A boy's wish was granted and he became known as Saint Nicholas and he would travel the world each Christmas Eve and deliver a gift of love to every boy and girl. He was given the Gift of Time to complete his task and he became the first person to visit a special place.

[1. Christmas--Fiction. 2. Santa Claus--Fiction. 3. The North Pole--Fiction. 4. Religion--Inspirational. 5. Family Values--Fiction.]
1. Title

The text was set in Goudy Old style.
The display type was set in Old English Text and Goudy Old Style.
The interior pages were printed on 80# Patina Matte.
The jacket wrap was printed on 100# stock with gloss laminate.
Production photography by Hans Kaczmarek, German Master Photographer and Son.
Color separations by Blackhawk Corporation.
Printed and bound by R.R. Donnelley & Sons Company.

PROLOGUE

Nicholas, as a boy, had a very unselfish wish.
He wanted to make children happy.
As a young man, one of his selfless acts of
love was witnessed by angels and his
wish was granted. He would become known
as Saint Nicholas and travel the world
each Christmas Eve and deliver a gift of
love to every boy and girl.

He was given the Gift of Time to make his
task possible, and he became the first
person to visit a very special place.

This is the continuing story of Saint Nicholas.
I know that it's true, because I was
there the whole time...

Mouka

Nicholas saw beautiful colored lights dancing in the sky as an Elf stepped from behind a tree. "Welcome to The Land Beyond Yon!" the Elf exclaimed. "We have been expecting you for a very long time." "Who are you?" asked Nicholas.

The Elf's name was Ono, and he told Nicholas that he was the mayor. Nicholas asked, "Where is The Land Beyond Yon?" Ono laughed. "It is right there" as he pointed to the lights. "All I see are colored lights in the sky," said Nicholas.

Ono explained that the colored lights were created by hundreds of prisms that create a dome. The dome makes it impossible to see where the Elves lived, unless of course, you know it's there. Some people think they are seeing the Northern Lights. One can only *see* the homes if they *believe* they are there. Nicholas trusted Ono and in the blink of an eye, the village appeared to Nicholas. "Oh it's truly beautiful!" Nicholas exclaimed.

9

Ono told Nicholas that the Elves had been there longer than anyone could remember. Their only job was to help fulfill children's wishes, which was all that they ever wanted to do. But this was not as easy as it seemed.

The Elves simply could not get along. Every day they would argue about most anything and everything. Also, something would go wrong almost every day. Sometimes the glue would be watered down and everything that had been glued that day would fall apart. On other days, tools would be missing and this would slow their work down. Each day would bring a new problem. Nicholas would need to solve these problems; after all, that was one of the big reasons he was there.

10

Nicholas was the very first person to visit The Land Beyond Yon.
The Elves were very excited to see him. They all cheered when
they first saw Nicholas....all except one. An Elf named Goe was
sweeping the floor when Nicholas entered the room. When he saw
Nicholas, all he said was "Humph!", and he turned his back and
continued sweeping. There was a rumor that the name **Goe** was
short for *Grouchy Old Elf.*

Nicholas noticed that there were several wagons, but none of them had wheels. Then he saw dozens of dolls, but none of them had heads. There were alphabet blocks on the shelves, but some letters were missing.

14

Nicholas asked one of the Elves why there were no blocks with the letters B or D on them. "I told *her* to do those letters!" said one Elf as he pointed to his friend on the other side of the bench. "You did not! I told *you* to do those letters!" exclaimed his friend. The Elves began to argue. Nicholas asked about the dolls and the answer was the same...more bickering!

15

Nicholas held a meeting with all the Elves. He told them
a story about two Elves who needed to move a wagon.
They went to opposite ends of the wagon and they both
pushed as hard as they could. They pushed and pushed
and pushed until they could push no more.

They decided that they were doing it all wrong. So, they went to opposite ends of the wagon and pulled as hard as they could, but the wagon would not move. They pulled and they pulled, but the wagon still would not move.

A wise old Elf had been watching. He explained that the
two Elves needed to work together. He gave them three
choices: both pull from one end, both push from one end,
or one push while the other pulls if they stood on opposite
ends. They took his advice and were surprised at how very
easy it was to move the wagon. He told the Elves that they
needed to work *with* each other, and not *against* each other.

18

The Elves knew Nicholas was right, and with that thought in mind, he began to organize their efforts. He assigned one Elf to make wheels for the wagons, one to make handles, one to make the wagon, and one to paint them. He organized all of the other groups as well. The Elves were very happy; not only were they accomplishing more, but they were having fun because they were *working together* and not just in the same room.

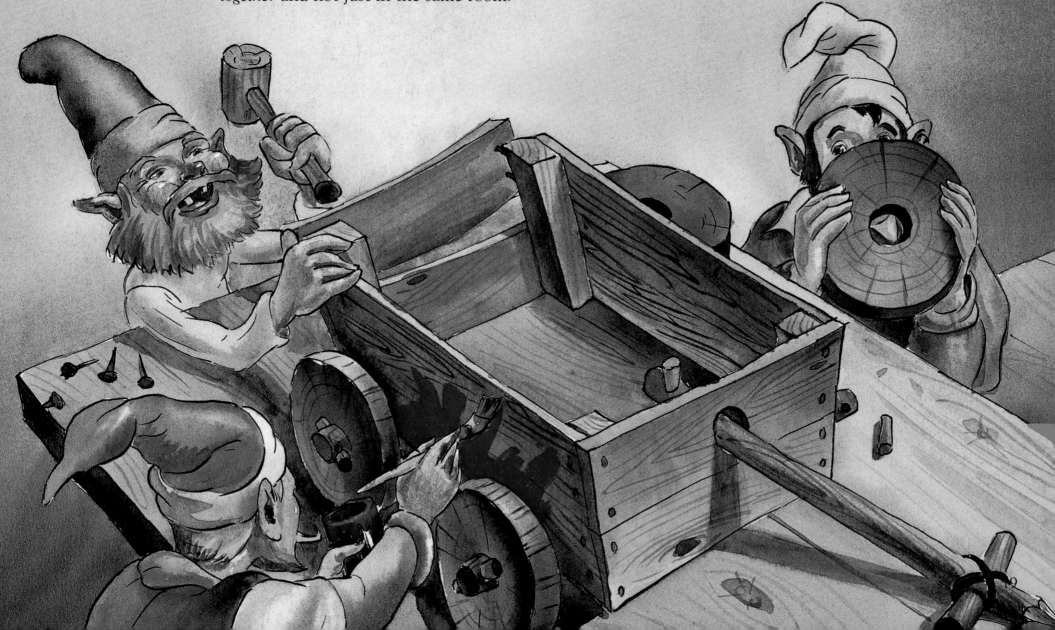

Nicholas went to the Wish Room. This is where he would sort out children's wishes from all over the world. When he saw how many gifts he would be delivering, he was amazed! Nicholas knew that a large sleigh would be needed to hold all the gifts.

He had several Elves build the most beautiful sleigh anyone had ever seen. Four silver bells were hung on each side of the sleigh.

22

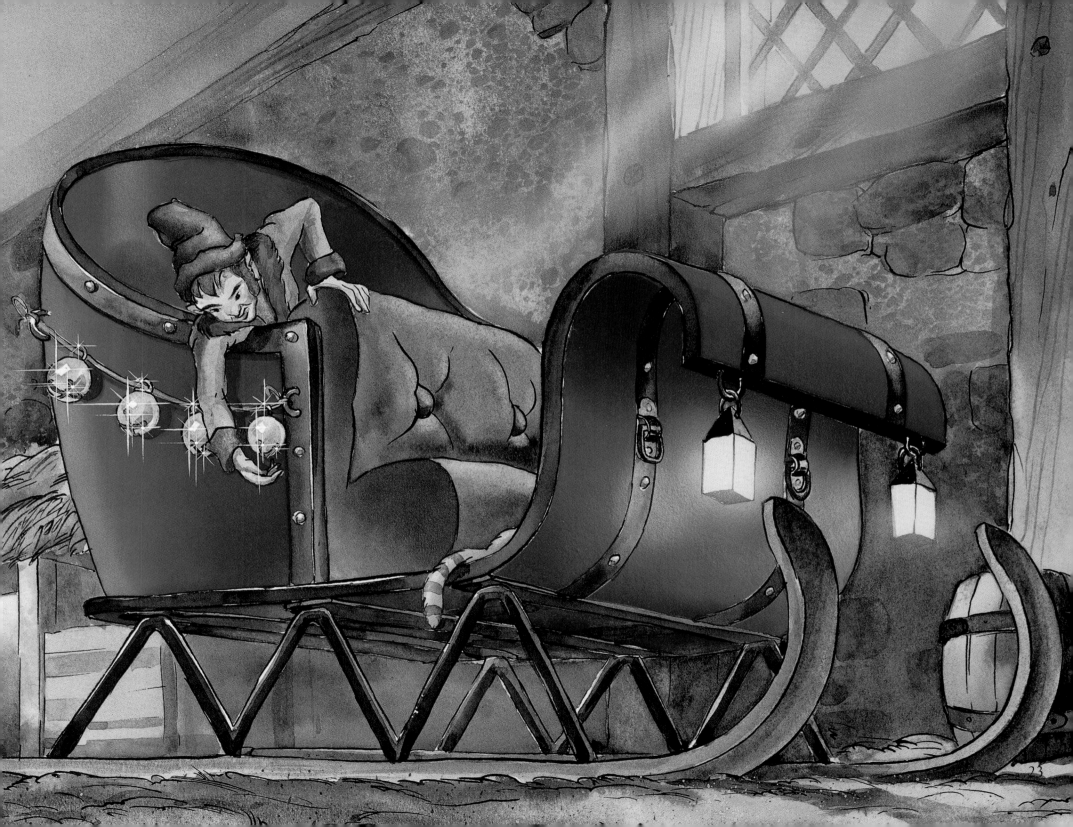

The next problem was clear. How would he pull such a big sleigh? He stood in the Wish Room staring out the window. There were eight reindeer outside! He brought the reindeer inside the barn and asked if they would help by pulling the sleigh. Of course, they nodded that they would.

Nicholas went back to the Wish Room to plan his Christmas Eve trip. How would he cross the oceans? He thought and he thought, but he just could not think of a solution.

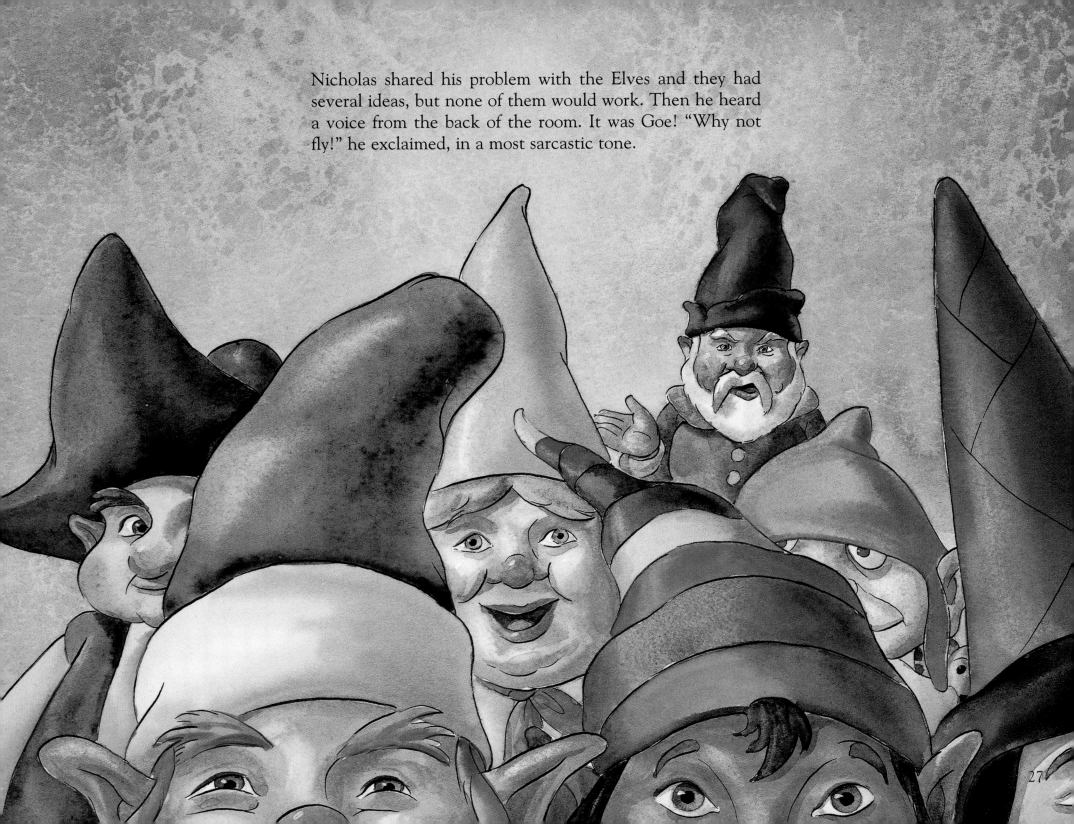

Nicholas shared his problem with the Elves and they had
several ideas, but none of them would work. Then he heard
a voice from the back of the room. It was Goe! "Why not
fly!" he exclaimed, in a most sarcastic tone.

27

"What a great idea!" Nicholas exclaimed. The Elves all cheered for Goe, but Goe was not at all happy. After all, he was being sarcastic and never intended to help Nicholas, or anyone else, for that matter.

Nicholas knew that all things are possible if you *believed*. So, the next morning, he went out to the barn to convince the reindeer that they could fly. They just stared at him. He fed them extra oats and told them that the oats would help them fly. Again, they stared blankly at him.

Goe was sweeping the barn floor and Nicholas noticed his reflection in the silver bells. He showed the bells to the reindeer and they really liked the reflections. He told the reindeer that the bells were magical. He tied one bell onto each reindeer's harness and told them that they were now able to fly. They really did *believe* it!

They seemed so sure of themselves that Nicholas climbed up onto the sleigh and shouted 'Up, up and away!', and away they did fly! Now, the bells really were not magical, but the reindeer thought that they were. They always could fly, they just never knew it. However, their *belief* in the silver bells made their flight possible, which means that maybe the silver bells were magical after all! In any case, Goe was *very* unhappy! He had helped again and he did not like it! Goe knew he would need to get even.

The days turned into weeks, and the weeks turned into months. Every day there were the same old problems of missing tools and watered down glue, but these things no longer deterred the Elves. Finally, it was Christmas Eve and all the Elves joined in loading the sleigh.

Ono ran up to Nicholas. One of the harnesses was missing! Everyone searched and searched, but they could not find the missing harness. One of the reindeer would not be able to go on the journey.

The youngest reindeer was smaller than the others and Nicholas told him that he could not go. The poor little reindeer was heartbroken and Nicholas felt very badly. "Who would do such a terrible deed!", Nicholas thought to himself.

Nicholas climbed up onto the sleigh and off he went. He was so upset that he did not notice that the silver bells were missing!

Meanwhile, Goe was peeking out from the barn and he was snickering. It was Goe who was causing all the problems and he was very pleased with himself! You see, Goe had never captured the *Spirit of Christmas*, even though he was surrounded by it.

The littlest reindeer walked up behind Goe and put his little head on Goe's shoulder. When he did this, one of his tiny little tears touched Goe's cheek and something wonderful happened!

The snow stopped for a moment and a bright *Light* appeared between
the clouds and it shone onto Goe. It was the Star of Bethlehem! The
Light filled Goe's heart with the *Spirit of Christmas*. Goe smiled for the
very first time and he wrapped his arms around the little reindeer.
"What have I done!", he said.

He told the reindeer not to worry, and that everything would be all right. Goe pulled the missing harness and bells from beneath a pile of hay.

44

He put the harness on the reindeer and climbed onto his back.
"Let us find Nicholas!", he exclaimed, and off they flew.

45

Nicholas had delivered thousands of gifts by the time
he arrived at the ocean and realized that the bells were
missing. At that very moment, he heard the jingle of
silver bells and he saw Goe with the little reindeer.

Goe explained what he had done and he apologized. Nicholas told Goe that he would need to help deliver the remaining gifts. Goe was grateful for the chance to redeem himself and he quickly hitched up the very happy little reindeer.

Nicholas and Goe then climbed up onto the sleigh. "Up, up and away!", Nicholas shouted, and away they flew. The only sounds were the jingle of the bells and the whoosh of cold air as they flew through the sky.

As they flew from rooftop to rooftop, Nicholas noticed a change in Goe. Goe was so happy that he began to sing! Why, he wasn't *Grouchy*....he was *Glad*!

Late Christmas Eve, they arrived home and all the Elves cheered. Ono ran over to Nicholas and exclaimed: "That is a job well done, and it took only one night!"

The Elves cheered for Goe as he climbed down off the sleigh. They did not cheer for what he had done, they cheered for what he had become! Once Goe had discovered the *Spirit of Christmas*, well, he just never could get that smile off his face. Nicholas, the Elves, and children all over the world celebrated Christmas. Nicholas and the Elves looked forward to the next day, for, as you know, making wishes come true was all that they ever wanted to do!

Acknowledgements

With special thanks to the many special friends and artists who have contributed to the publication of this Limited First Edition of "The Nicholas Stories: The First Flight of Saint Nicholas".

A special thanks to Harry Knights for the labor of his love, and to Christine Knights, an excellent Elf and special friend, to Betty and Harry Knights, Jr. for their loyal and enthusiastic support. To Charlie Flood for staying the course; to Roger and Doris Hefler, Phil Testa, Steve Gonzalez, Vicent and Mahruh Neville, Henry Scheuring, Jim and Doris Courchaine and Andrew Rigrod, all who in their special way, saw the vision as it turned into reality.

To Tom and Claudia Burton, Joel Faynor, Chavdar Chushev, and all the Calico Creations' crew, whose beautiful paintings tell a story within our story.

To Hans Kaczmarek, Master German Photographer and Son, whose knowledge of film, the love of art and the persistence to capture the color palette and illumination of our paintings.

To the entire staff of Blackhawk Corporation, whose trained eyes and technical expertise brought to life the brilliance of our paintings.

To Lou and JoAnn Rotunno, Patrick and Nancy Keenan, George and Edwina Worsley, Yoshiro and Sueko Oishi, Alison and Beth Donovan, Norman Godheim, Randy DeFazio, Thomas Rotunno, Alice and Jacklyn Schmetzer, Stephanie and Richard Gehring, Rebecca Womble, Elizabeth Rotunno, Mark Mazzone, Linda Hyer, Jill Ressler, Mark Kasrel, Kevin and Karen Hand, Robert and Josephine Tomasulo, Sheila Wessner, Amy McCallum, Rene Gandelman, Michael Long, Brad McKinney, Ralph and Patricia Rotunno, Harriet Segal, Thomas Steele, Mike Brown, Jan Kenny and family, Kathy Gomberg, Al Golden, James Petroff, James Edmonson, Warren Schmidt, Richard and Ellen Stupak, David West, James and Bonnie Parsons, Ross Hagstoc, Henry and Christine Coleman, James McDade, Anthony Latona, Edna Sheilds, Harold Markle, Steven Passion, Brad Yoder, Leonard Platnick, Marcus Barth, Vito and Jean Magarelli, Dante S. Alberi, Darlene Calzon-Barror, Christopher Ferguson, James Rowe, Lawrence Kirsch, Gerald Weinberg, and, David J. Levenson.

In Loving Memory of Roger H. Hefler, co-founder of Studio City Holding, partner and special friend.

To my guardian angels, Martha, Gurnie and Ona, whose presence lights the path.

And with more thanks than I can express, to Audrey and Lauren, whose love and smiles inspired this publication, and, to Ginny for her relentless love and guiding force.

Larry D. Faw

54

The Nicholas Stories:

"The Boy With A Wish"
"The First Flight of Saint Nicholas"
"The Maiden Voyage of Kris Kringle"

Zweig Knights Publishing Corporation
copyright, 1998, 1997, 1994 & 1970™
the end...

56